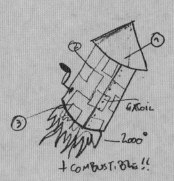

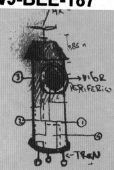

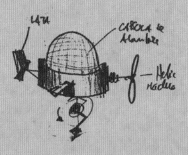

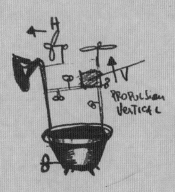

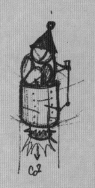

CAPTAIN ARSENIO

INVENTIONS AND (MIS)ADVENTURES IN FLIGHT

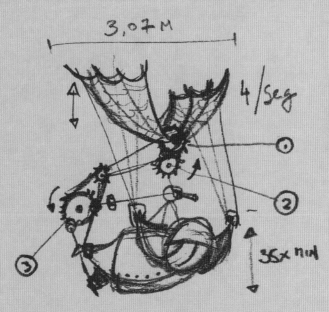

written & illustrated by

PABLO BERNASCONI

Houghton Mifflin Company

Boston 2005

THE RESULT OF LOOKING UP

Flight, one of the most ancient wishes ever known, has inspired hundreds of fantastic creations. From Icarus to the Wright brothers, history has seen thousands of adventurers who have felt the dangerous urge to soar with the birds. This passionate impulse has resulted in many failures.

Scientists, philosophers, doctors, and even crazy people all have been pioneers of aviation, and each has made a different contribution—sometimes right, sometimes wrong—to the pursuit of flight. This is the story of one such man.

THE END AND THE BEGINNING

Manuel J. Arsenio was a careless cheese master, blacksmith, scuba diver, and ship captain. Though he was given the easiest of missions in each of these careers, he still couldn't complete any of them successfully. This problem may be the reason he left those jobs behind to enter the distinguished pages of aviation history.

One day in 1782, Captain Arsenio decided to build the first in a long series of eccentric projects that would change his life. And although he had little knowledge of physics or mechanics and had access only to useless materials, he demonstrated great patience and determination throughout the course of his flight experiments.

> "My days of sailing and scuba-diving are over; I retire with grace to begin a new stage in my life that will undoubtedly go down in history. I'm going to achieve what has been humanity's desire for centuries: I will build a flying machine."
> —CAPTAIN ARSENIO, MAY 1, 1782

THE DISCOVERY

How do we know about Captain Arsenio? His diary was found by chance just one year ago, under circumstances to be discussed later. In its ninety pages full of doodles, notes, and technical writings, Arsenio developed eighteen different designs for a flying machine, each one original, foolish, and fantastic. Here we explore six of the eighteen most influential projects that have contributed to modern aviation.

Captain Arsenio's diary is the oldest and most precious aviation manuscript ever known, second only to Leonardo da Vinci's. Fortunately, the text is still legible and Arsenio's notes, diagrams, and ideas take us back in time to reveal the hidden mystery of the inventor's thoughts.

"Why can birds fly and we humans cannot? What cruel destiny stops all people from seeing the world from above, tasting the clouds, and undoing long distances by air?"
—CAPTAIN ARSENIO, JUNE 7, 1783

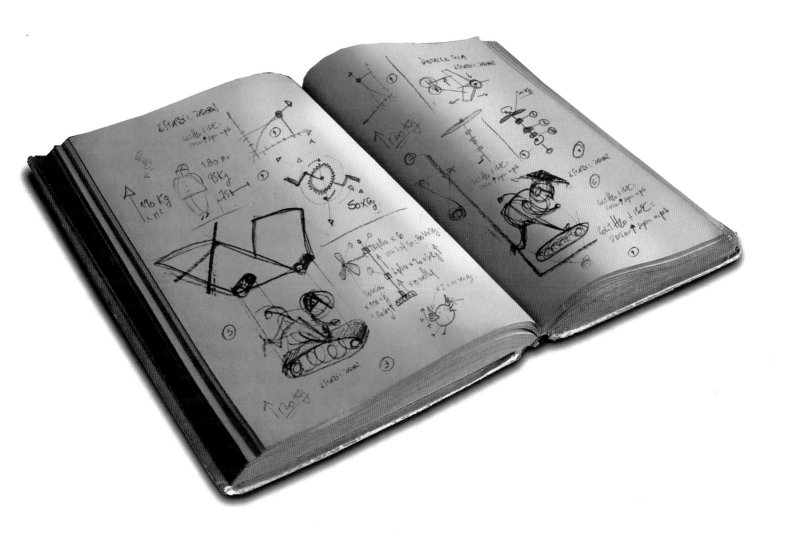

PROJECT NUMBER I: MOTOCANARY

The Motocanary was an ingenious experiment that demanded a lot of work. Evidently, it was harder for Captain Arsenio to find enough birds and tie them together with a rope than it was to achieve flight. Although the discovery was revolutionary, it took two days to get the captain down from the tree in which he was stuck.

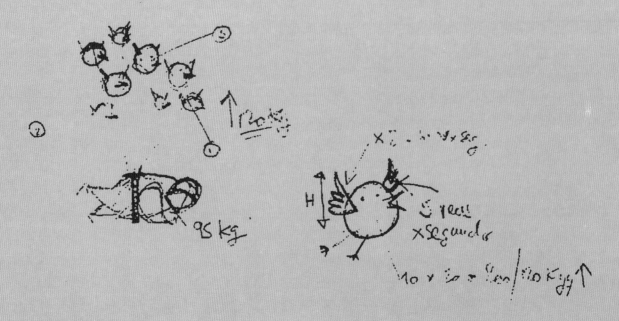

"Carts are dragged along by horses, sleighs by dogs, and plows by bulls. I think that if I concentrate enough birds together, the sustaining force will help me win the clouds. It cannot fail!"
—CAPTAIN ARSENIO, FEBRUARY 18, 1784

FLIGHT DIARY

1 The selection process is demanding and exhausting. I accept only those who have wings.

2 I start running, and the birds accept the challenge. The glory is mine, mine!

3 My feet leave the ground and I have control of the height. My bones feel the change. I'm almost another bird.

Phase 1: 14 hrs   Phase 2: 10 min   Phase 3: 4.5 sec

NOTE: As improbable as it appears, this diary shows us that the Motocanary did fly for a few feet before crashing into a tree

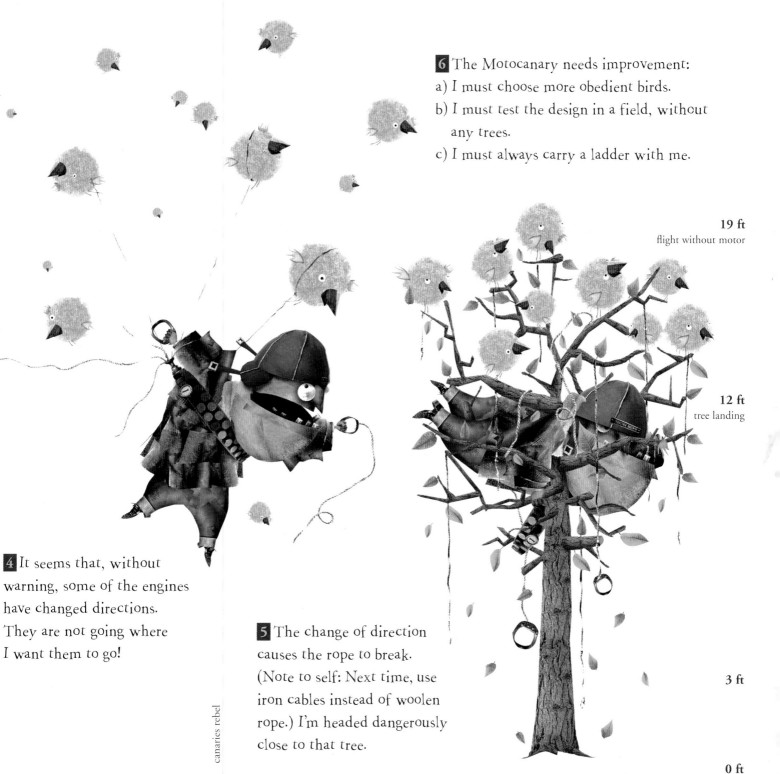

6 The Motocanary needs improvement:

a) I must choose more obedient birds.

b) I must test the design in a field, without any trees.

c) I must always carry a ladder with me.

19 ft
flight without motor

12 ft
tree landing

4 It seems that, without warning, some of the engines have changed directions. They are not going where I want them to go!

canaries rebel

5 The change of direction causes the rope to break. (Note to self: Next time, use iron cables instead of woolen rope.) I'm headed dangerously close to that tree.

3 ft

0 ft

Phase 4: 2 sec   Phase 5: 1 sec   phase 6: total elapsed time: 2 days, 14 hrs, 10 min, 7.5 sec

Maybe the failure is due to Captain Arsenio's misplaced trust in the unreliable canaries.

PROJECT NUMBER 2: FLYING RUNNER

Good cardiovascular health would become a determining factor in Captain Arsenio's second ambition. The acceleration of the runner would allow—according to his plans—the wings to beat up and down in imitation of a bird's flight and lift the machine off the ground. The direction control is unknown.

"I can leave the ground by the effort of an energetic run, transferred
to the little wings and multiplied thirty times by the transfer pulleys.
Running + wings = access to heaven. It cannot fail!"
—CAPTAIN ARSENIO, MARCH 23, 1785

FLIGHT DIARY

1 Countdown to zero. I'm preparing for the big run. I've got faith.

2 I start the acceleration, and the wings seem to be in working order. But I'm not elevating yet.

3 The machine starts to rise at maximum speed. I'm starting to get very tired.

4 All systems go, the balance is controlled—the prototype is a success...up until this point.

| Phase 1: at rest | Phase 2: 21 min | Phase 3: 47 sec | Phase 4: 1 min |

NOTE: The reader may notice that there are significant differences between what is written and what actually happened. Thi

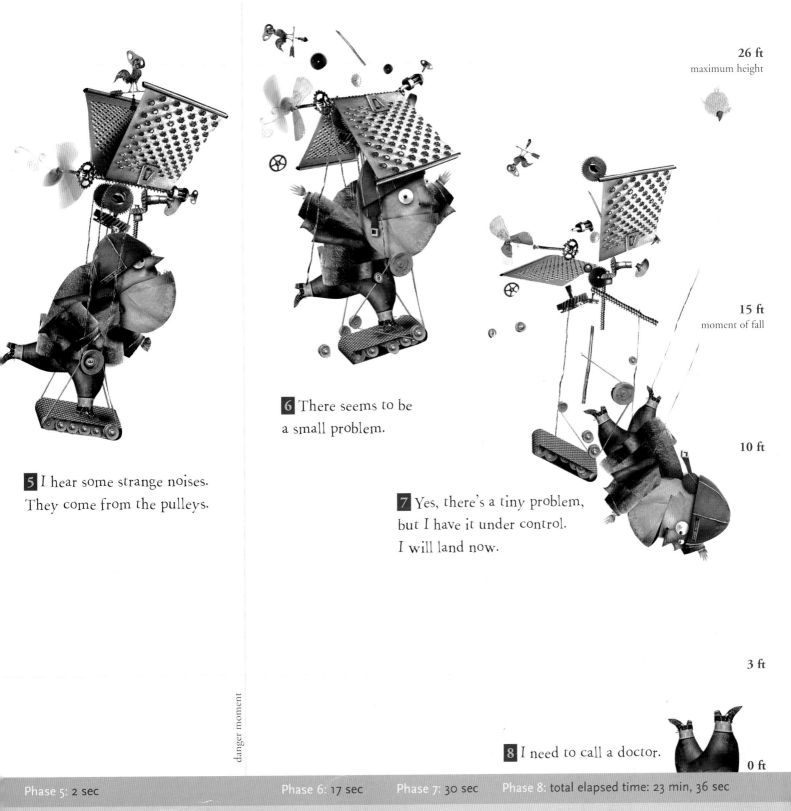

26 ft
maximum height

15 ft
moment of fall

10 ft

5 I hear some strange noises. They come from the pulleys.

6 There seems to be a small problem.

7 Yes, there's a tiny problem, but I have it under control. I will land now.

danger moment

3 ft

8 I need to call a doctor.

0 ft

Phase 5: 2 sec   Phase 6: 17 sec   Phase 7: 30 sec   Phase 8: total elapsed time: 23 min, 36 sec

may be due to Captain Arsenio's unflagging optimism (or the many bumps on the head that he suffered from his experiments).

PROJECT NUMBER 3: CORKSCREWPTERUS

No one knows what was going through Captain Arsenio's mind when he conceived of this contraption. What we do know is that he placed so much emphasis on getting off the ground that he forgot a substantial part of the matter: how to keep himself in the air. Obvious results.

"All past propelling mechanisms were wrong. I need to find a way to beat gravity, despite my generous weight. The compression of two metal springs should do the trick; I anticipate a big leap. But I will put little wings on my back, just in case. It cannot fail!"

—CAPTAIN ARSENIO, NOVEMBER 15, 1785

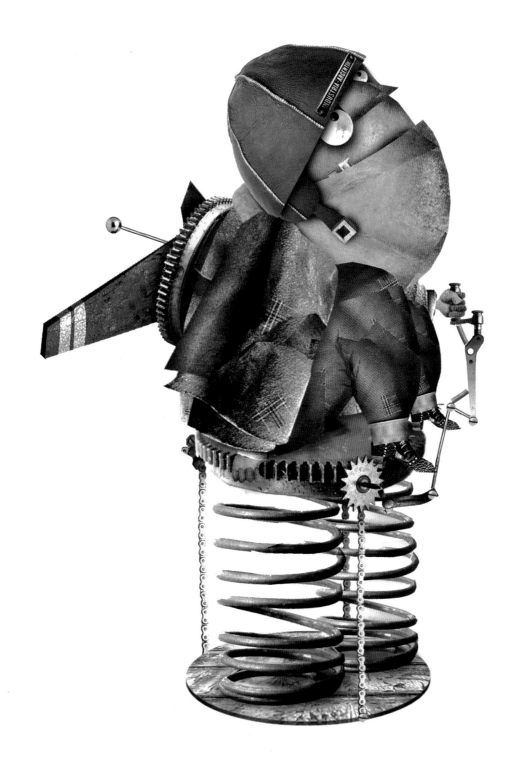

FLIGHT DIARY

3 Oh!!!! The acceleration is violent, and I've conquered gravity without any problems.

2 I start the countdown: 10, 9, 8, 7, 6, 5, 4, 3, 2, 1

1 Everything is ready for takeoff. The jump is possible.

Phase 1: at rest Phase 2: 10 sec Phase 3: 3.5 sec

NOTE: This document is the only one of its kind; there is no other recorded data of a person surviving such a fall, either

4 I've already passed through the clouds; I start the controlled descent.

5 Now it is time for the wings.

99 ft

6 Descent is completely under control, although the wings do not respond as I had expected.

50 ft

panic point

3 ft

7 The doctor is not at home. I will call the veterinarian.

0 ft

Phase 4: 1 min   Phase 5: 1 sec   Phase 6: 7.25 sec   Phase 7: total elapsed time: 1 min, 21.75 sec

efore or since.

PROJECT NUMBER 4: AERIAL SUBMARINE

This is one of the rare occasions when—due to the obvious physical similarities with the submarine of Arsenio's time—we can verify the nautical history of our hero's past. However, the Aerial Submarine actually possessed the virtues (and defects) of what would later be known as the blimp. Through the use of a hydrogen-filled compartment, the machine did get lighter and float through the air. The problem was that this gas was very flammable and the flight vessel was made of wood. The results leave little to the imagination.

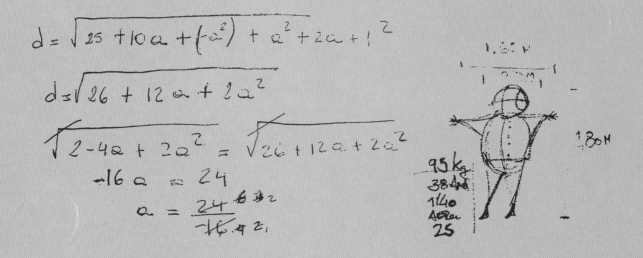

$$d = \sqrt{25 + 10a + (-a^2)} + a^2 + 2a + 1^2$$

$$d = \sqrt{26 + 12a + 2a^2}$$

$$\sqrt{2 - 4a + 2a^2} = \sqrt{26 + 12a + 2a^2}$$

$$-16a = 24$$

$$a = \frac{24}{-16}$$

95 kg
38
140
A
25

"By mixing sulfuric acid with iron, I obtain a miraculous gas with which I will float like a balloon. But this time, I will take advantage of my nautical knowledge to better control the flight direction. Victory is mine! It cannot fail!"

—CAPTAIN ARSENIO, APRIL 27, 1786

FLIGHT DIARY

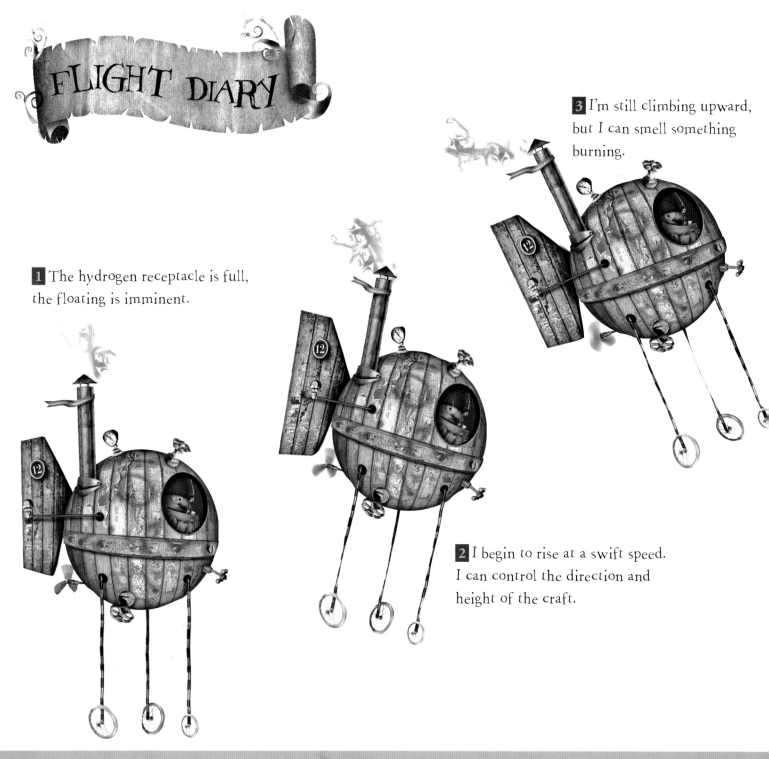

1 The hydrogen receptacle is full, the floating is imminent.

2 I begin to rise at a swift speed. I can control the direction and height of the craft.

3 I'm still climbing upward, but I can smell something burning.

Phase 1: at rest   Phase 2: 8.25 sec   Phase 3: 4 sec

NOTE: A complex way to demonstrate a total unawareness of the laws of physics. This flight diary also shows us how Arseni

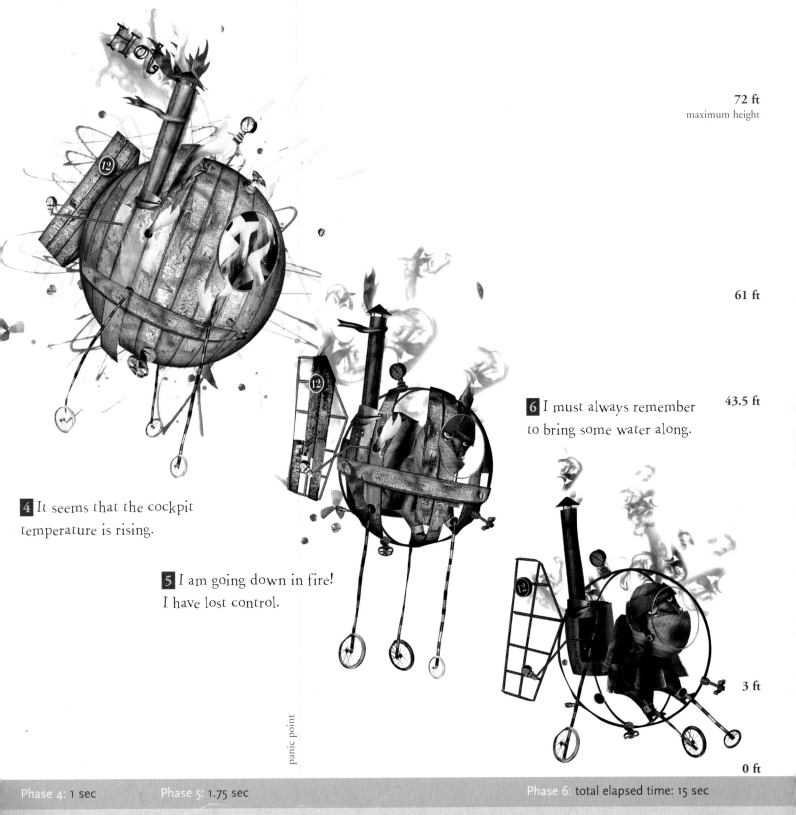

72 ft
maximum height

61 ft

4 It seems that the cockpit temperature is rising.

5 I am going down in fire! I have lost control.

6 I must always remember to bring some water along.

43.5 ft

panic point

3 ft

0 ft

ame by his excessive and somewhat permanent tan.

PROJECT NUMBER 5: THE ILLUSION BURNER

This apparatus is a precursor to the modern turbine engine. With initial success, the captain was able to combine fuel and compressed hot air, generating a forceful expulsion of gases. But however positive Arsenio may have been about the Illusion Burner at the outset, the hole left in the ground tells another story.

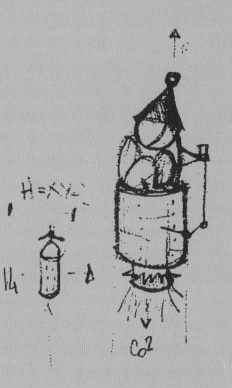

"I have discovered that the compression of gases in a compartment, stimulated by four small fans, is as powerful as a stampede of bulls. If only I could control it and guide it in one direction... I see stars in my future. It cannot fail!"
—CAPTAIN ARSENIO, JANUARY 5, 1787

FLIGHT DIARY

3 EHHHHAAAAUUUUHHH!
I feel my brain inside my feet!
I hadn't planned on rising
up this quickly — or leaving
the flying machine on
the ground.

2 Nine, eight, seven — perhaps
I should have tested the machine
with a rat first? — six, five —
I hope that smell is normal —
four, three — that noise *can't* be
normal — two, one — I'd better
get out of this.

1 Gas receptacles are
full, the ventilators on.
Ignition!

Phase 1: at rest   Phase 2: 19 sec   Phase 3: .025 sec

NOTE: Note the chin strap on the special helmet used for this experiment. It is one of the reasons that Arsenio could tur

4 The energy source was a complete success, and the ascent was as forceful as a shot. Probably the damage will be, too.

5 The descent up to here is completely under control and predictable. I also predict that I will crash over those rocks . . .

204 ft
descent without control ▼

50 ft

moment in which the project receives its name

6 Miraculously, the landing was better than what I expected. I'll try to see if I can recover any piece of the machine.

3 ft

0 ft

Phase 4: 1 min   Phase 5: 12 sec

Phase 6: total elapsed time: 1 min, 31.025 sec

his head only to the right.

PROJECT NUMBER 6: HAMSTERTRONIC

In the mid-1780s, there were very few alternatives to motor-driven propulsion: electricity was still in the experimental stages, gasoline was expensive and hard to get, and the steam engine presented problems in that it was so large and heavy. The Hamstertronic solved these problems. However, for some strange reason, parts of this apparatus ended up in a forgotten tent in the Moscow circus.

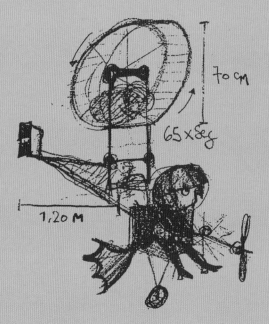

"This engine will solve the energy riddle. If an adult hamster runs on the wheel carousel at a rate of nine turns per second, I can multiply it mechanically without problems into the vertical movement of the machine. As for the direction... the wind will decide it. It cannot fail!"

—CAPTAIN ARSENIO, AUGUST 15, 1787

1 The riddle is solved. With the help of my little friend, I'll float in the air as a ship in the water. Brilliant.

3 Everything is going well and I own the sky. But is the hamster trying to tell me something?

2 Come on, little fellow! Four, five, six, seven, eight... my sensors point to nine turns per second. The calculation was right and I rise upward, full of hope.

| Phase 1: at rest | Phase 2: 9 sec | Phase 3: 2 min |

NOTE: While the Hamstertronic was not a success, this invention marks the first parachute escape of an animal.

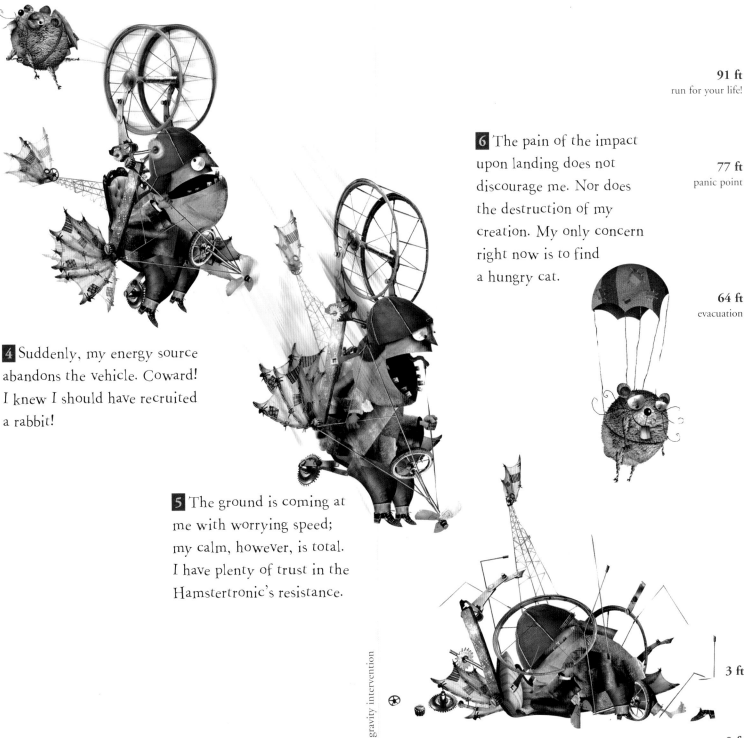

91 ft
run for your life!

6 The pain of the impact upon landing does not discourage me. Nor does the destruction of my creation. My only concern right now is to find a hungry cat.

77 ft
panic point

64 ft
evacuation

4 Suddenly, my energy source abandons the vehicle. Coward! I knew I should have recruited a rabbit!

5 The ground is coming at me with worrying speed; my calm, however, is total. I have plenty of trust in the Hamstertronic's resistance.

gravity intervention

3 ft

0 ft

GOODBYE FROM BELOW

As it happens with almost all legends, multiple versions contradict one another, proof disappears, and word of mouth constructs stories that differ greatly from the reality. No one knows for certain exactly what happened to Captain Arsenio and his flying machines; all that is left is his diary—ninety pages of consecutive failures—and one big question: Did he eventually succeed?

Some say that Arsenio's book was buried near Cairo, Egypt—7,508 miles away from where he lived in Patagonia, Argentina. Others disagree and tell us it was in a chest at the bottom of the sea, buried under a pile of rusty metal junk. But most people insist with determination that Captain Arsenio's diary was found on the surface of the moon on July 20, 1969.

"Many years have passed since that first Motocanary. Although I have failed many times, I have learned so much. And today, for the first time, I am sure that this new machine I have developed is going to work. I deserve a piece of heaven, and I am going for it!"
—CAPTAIN ARSENIO, DECEMBER 6, 1789